Hi, I'm CHIP!

Shirley Winkle Barton

Interior Graphics Design by:
Jared Beckstrand

AuthorHouse™
1663 Liberty Drive
Bloomington, IN 47403
www.authorhouse.com
Phone: 833-262-8899

Because of the dynamic nature of the Internet, any web addresses or links contained in this book may have changed since publication and may no longer be valid. The views expressed in this work are solely those of the author and do not necessarily reflect the views of the publisher, and the publisher hereby disclaims any responsibility for them.

Any people depicted in stock imagery provided by Getty Images are models, and such images are being used for illustrative purposes only.
Certain stock imagery © Getty Images.

This book is printed on acid-free paper.

ISBN: 979-8-8230-3593-4 (sc)
ISBN: 979-8-8230-3595-8 (hc)
ISBN: 979-8-8230-3594-1 (e)

Library of Congress Control Number: 2024921875

Print information available on the last page.

Published by AuthorHouse

authorHOUSE®

This book is dedicated
to my late husband Brent.
He loved Chip and Chip
loved him. They spent
all their time together
and Chip took real good
care of Grandpa. They
were amazing companions
and mischievous buddies.

Hi! My name is Chip.
I'm a Labradoodle.
My friends call me Chipper,
but my best friends call me

Chip The Dip.

Let me tell you my story.

When I was a puppy I went home with a family I loved. I ran and chased my best friend Hudson.

We rolled around and played tug-o-war with my toys. I usually won the tugging,

but the best part was sleeping in his bed every night.

His mom helped me learn things... important things like how to play outside.

I learned how to ring a bell when I needed to go out. So easy for everyone.

How to sit and lay down. How to sit and walk on her left side so I wouldn't trip her.

But one thing she couldn't change was my barking and jumping when I saw new friends.

So excited.....

Sometimes they would take me to Grandpa's house to play.

I loved going there.

We would play in Grandpa's ginormous backyard or I would just sit on Grandpa's lap.

One day we went to Grandpa's house to play. When they went home they didn't take me.

I wasn't sure what was happening, but my food and all my toys were there.

Confused, I jumped up on Grandpa's lap and we just sat there.

I didn't know if he
thought I was sad, but
he let me sleep in his bed
that night and every
night after.

I think he liked it
as much as I did.

The next day we had so much fun.
He let me have food from the table.
I knew it was naughty
        but so so yummy.

We sat outside in the sun and
he would throw the ball.

Sometimes I would play with
Biggie the tortoise while
Grandpa was napping.

Some days we would
walk and get the
mail. Well, he would
walk and I would

Run - Run - Run.

Sometimes in the summer we drove to the cabin for a couple days. He would sit on the porch and watch me and I would run and dig in the dirt.

There were squirrels and birds to chase.

Sometimes if I was quiet we would see deer and sometimes there would be a baby deer. I didn't chase the deer because they were big and scary.

After a while Grandpa seemed to get a little slower. He stopped going to the mailbox as often and playing catch in the yard as often.

But we still sat in the sun and napped.

There were days when my cousins came to play.

June...   Benny...   and Ruth.

Three
little dachshund doggies.

June didn't play with me.
She just wanted to watch Biggie
the tortoise.

Sometimes June would jump in the koi pond and swim. Benny didn't want to play either.

He would run and bark and chase the birds.

But not Ruth!! She came to play.

We ran and played and hid
in the bushes. We played so
hard and fast that we had to
rest sometimes.

Boy, I love that Ruth.

After we played
we all got a treat.

Yummy, Yummy, Treat.

Then they would go home
and Grandpa and I would nap.

I noticed Grandpa wasn't walking so much or wanting to play ball.

He only wanted to sit in the backyard and hold me on his lap.

He would pet me and talk to me. He was napping a lot.

Seemed like he was staying in bed more but still let me be with him.

One day all my family
and cousins came to visit.
I had so much fun playing
with everyone and I was
held a lot.

I was so excited.

Then one day
Grandpa was gone.
I looked all over
for him.

    In his bed.

Outside in our
favorite place
to sit in the
sun.

Out in
the street
by the
mailbox.

    He was gone, just gone.

I could hear my family saying...

"What about Chip? Where is he going to go?"

I was so confused. Why did I need to go anywhere? I loved living with Grandpa.

I got sad and didn't want to play or go outside.

Not sure what was going to happen to me.

One day weeks later two of
my family came to visit.
Oddly the next day I was in
the car with them with my
toys and food...even my bed.
We drove for a very long time...
hours and hours and hours.

I had no idea where
we were going.
I felt nervous and
kind of scared.

Finally we stopped and they let me out of the car. The ground was covered with really cold stuff.

I found out later it was snow. Not sure what to do, I ran to the door. When the door opened someone said...

"Welcome to Utah Chipper!"

I recognized these people.
They were my family who would
visit Grandpa. This was my
new home! Lots of people,
but best of all I have a big
brother BILLY.

And I mean **BIG** brother.

He is a Malinois.

This is a wonderful family
to love me.

We go on long walks and
play in the park.

They throw the ball and
Billy and I chase it.

Billy is really fast so I don't get
the ball very often. I love spending
time with them.

Sometimes we go
visit my cousin Smidge.
She is a chihuahua.
She lives at Truxton
and Brighton's house.

Smidge is kind of sassy
so I mostly play
with Truxton.

He likes to run and jump
so we have lots of fun.

My favorite friend is Wynn.
We spend all of our time together.
She is 11 and takes such good
care of me.
She gives me
a bath and
combs my hair.

One time she
made me an
outfit to wear.
That was strange
but she had fun.

She carries me all the time and
gives me yummy cheese.

But best of all
she lets me sleep
with her just
like Grandpa.

I know my family
was sad for me when
I had to leave, but I
love my new home.

I miss Grandpa and
all our fun every day.

But I love my life in
Utah.

Wynn and her family
make me very happy.

The End

Printed in the United States
by Baker & Taylor Publisher Services